not drawn by **Pam Smallcomb**   not written by **Robert Weinstock**

schwartz & wade books · new york

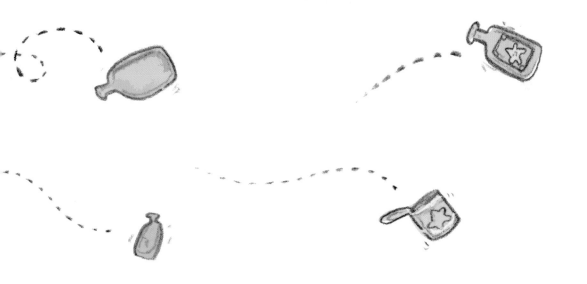

Sometimes I wonder if my friend Evelyn is from Mars.

PLEASE DON'T
KICK THE FLOWERS

She's not one single bit ordinary.

And she's a little
mysterious.

I'm not.

Evelyn is up on all the latest fashion trends.

I'm not.

If Evelyn was a car, she would get a speeding ticket.

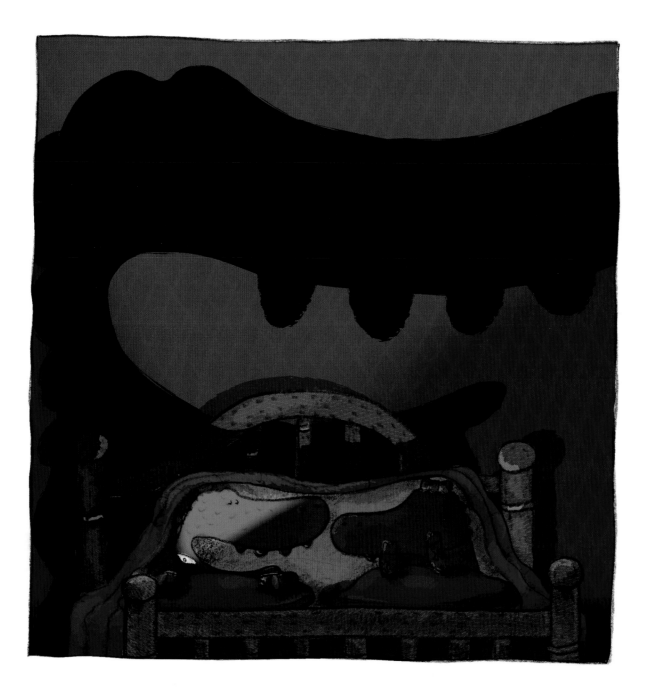

If Evelyn was a book, you'd read her all night under the covers to see what happened next.

My mom says Evelyn is a jumping bean.

Most of the time, **I'm not.**

When Evelyn comes over,
she changes my room.

My scales.

And my pet worm.

She's a wonderful decorator.

I'm not.

In school, Evelyn drew a portrait of Ms. Stacy with her chocolate milk.
And made a statue of Mr. Milton from old bubble gum.

Evelyn says she's just recycling,
but I think she's an artist.

I, most definitely, am *not*.

Evelyn is lots of things.

Circus performer.

I'm not.

Antarctic explorer.

EUREKA!!

I'm not.

WHY AM I ALWAYS THE PENGUIN?

Queen of England.

I'm not . . .

I'm not . . .

I'm not.

Evelyn sits down
next to me.

She says, "I'm stinky
at spelling."

"I'm crummy
at karate."

I'm not.

"I'm scared of the dark."

I'm not.

"I'm the absolute worst at making cookies."

A friend who is always by her side.

Through thick and thin.

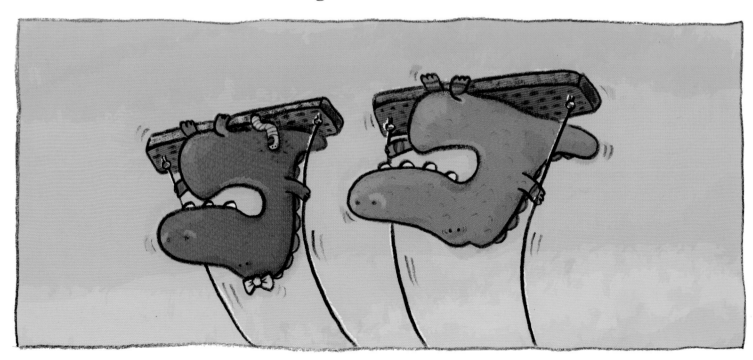

A true-blue friend.

Evelyn sighs. "Is there anyone in the whole wide world like that?"

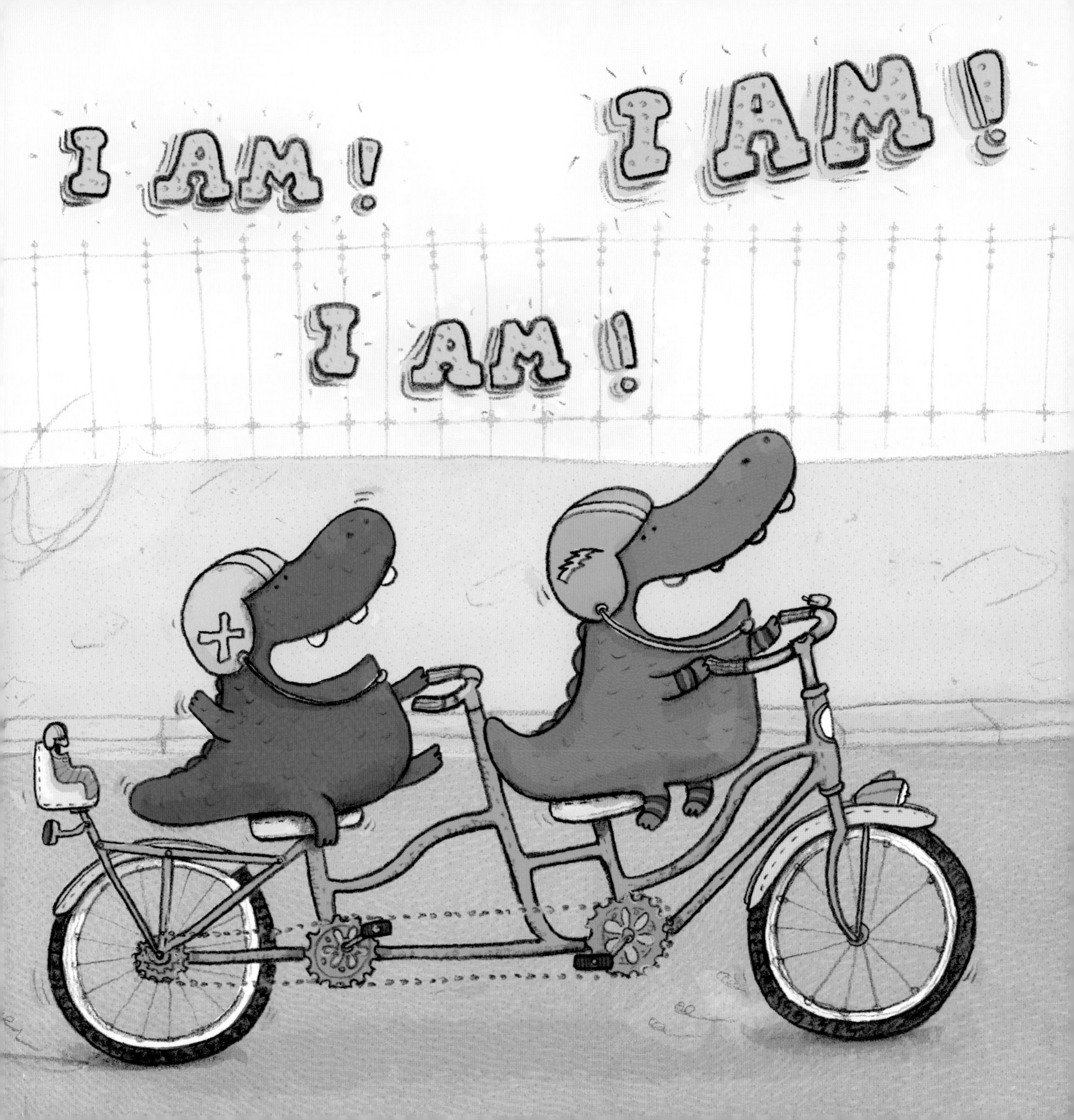
I AM!
I AM!
I AM!

I am exactly like that!

To Chris, Amy, Alex, Caitlin, Patrick, and Lucas with love.
And to the amazing James Proimos, über-wunderkind.
Special thanks to Ann Kelley for pulling it all together.
—P.S.

For Justine . . . who is!
—R.W.

Visit us on the Web! www.randomhouse.com/kids

Educators and librarians, for a variety of teaching tools, visit us at www.randomhouse.com/teachers

Library of Congress Cataloging-in-Publication Data
Smallcomb, Pam. ★ I'm not / Pam Smallcomb ; illustrated by Robert Weinstock.—1st ed. ★ p. cm. ★ Summary: A young
girl discovers that best friends can enjoy and do well at different things as long as they are good at being friends.
ISBN 978-0-375-86115-4 (trade) — ISBN 978-0-375-96115-1 (glb) ★ [1. Individuality—Fiction. 2. Best friends—Fiction.
3. Friendship—Fiction.] I. Weinstock, Robert, ill. II. Title. III. Title: I am not. ★ PZ7.S6375Iag 2011 ★ [E]—dc22
2009046742

The text of this book is set in Lomba.

The illustrations were not rendered in watercolor or woodcut . . . but were super fun to make anyway!

Book design by Rachael Cole

MANUFACTURED IN CHINA
10 9 8 7 6 5 4 3 2 1
First Edition

JE Smallcomb
5/11/BT

DISCARD

DATE DUE

JUL 0 6 2011		
AUG 1 2 2011		
SEP.-0 9 2011		
SEP 2 8 201		
OCT 2 0 2011		

Demco, Inc. 38-293